WIZZO
and the
COOKIE BABIES

Wizzo
and
the Cookie Babies

written and illustrated
by Gina Calleja

Napoleon Publishing

Published by Napoleon Publishing Inc.
Toronto, Ontario, Canada

Printed in Canada

Canadian Cataloguing in Publication Data

Calleja, Gina
    Wizzo and the cookie babies

I. Title.

PS8555.A512W59 1994   jC813'.54   C94-931071-9
PZ7.C35Wii   1994

For Marcel and Antoine

Wizzo the Wizard, who lived on the moon, was sitting one day in his kitchen.
He had nothing to do.
He was bored.

His wife was away on a trip. Before she left, she had said, "Wizzo, you've been working too hard. You must take it easy, put your feet up, have a rest."

"Yes, Winnie," said Wizzo. "But I'd rather go on a trip."

Ms. Wizzo had pretended not to hear this.

His wife had been away for a week. In that time, Wizzo had made spells for people who needed them. He had read all the books in the library. He had done all the chores. He had worked in the garden. He had taken Wuff the dog for long walks.
Now he had nothing to do.
He was very bored.

He sighed. "Let me think."
After a few minutes, he said, "I'll bake some cookies."
He searched through *Winnie's Wonderful Bakery Book*, looking for a cookie recipe.
"Pies... puddings... cakes... cookies... Here we are!"

Then he went to buy what he needed.
He bought flour, salt, sugar, margarine,
eggs and raisins.
He bought a cookie cutter as well.

"Looks as if you're going to do a lot of baking," said the cashier. "That's seven dollars and eighty-five cents, please."
Wizzo took out his wallet. "Oh dear," he said. "I only have seven dollars and eighty cents. May I owe it till next week, or shall I cast a spell for five cents?"
"I can wait," said the cashier. "I trust you."

When he got home, Wizzo took out all the mixing bowls, spoons and baking pans and set to work.

But he couldn't find his glasses.

"I don't need them," he said. "Now then... " and he read the recipe.

Twelve cups margarine
Twelve cups sugar
Twelve cups flour
Twelve cups raisins
Pinch of salt
Eggs

Eggs? The recipe was smudged and Wizzo
couldn't see how many eggs were needed.
"Well, I bought two dozen. May as well use
the lot," and he mixed in the eggs, shells
and all.
He rolled out the mixture and cut it with
the new cookie cutter. He filled twelve
baking trays with cookies.

Wizzo's oven had four shelves, so he put in four trays.

He sat down. "I'll count to one hundred. The cookies should be done by then."

So he counted. By the time he got to ninety, the cookies smelled so good that he took them out of the oven.

He poked them to see if they were done. "Perfect," he said, and he opened the oven and put in four more trays.

"One, two, three... "
There was a knock on the front door. Wizzo
went to see who was there.
After several minutes, Wizzo came back
into the kitchen and began to count again.
When he reached one hundred, he took the
cookies out of the oven.
He poked them to see if they were done.
"Perfect," he said.

Wizzo put the last four trays in the oven.
He yawned.
"I feel a bit tired now," he said. "I think I'll
stretch out for awhile."
He lay down on the couch and fell fast asleep.
Fifteen minutes later, he woke up with a start.
"My cookies!" he cried, and he ran to the
oven to take them out.
He poked them to see if they were done.
"Perfect," he said.

Then Wizzo looked at all the cookies. He counted them.

One hundred and forty-four cookies.

"That's funny," he said. "I made twelve dozen cookies. Winnie only makes half a dozen with that recipe."

He scratched the top of his head and found his glasses up there. He checked the recipe book.

"Half a cup of margarine, half a cup of sugar, half a cup of flour. Oh!"

He knew now what a mistake he had made.

"Never mind," he said. "They look too good
to eat. They're so cute I wish they were real.
Well, I can fix that!"
He made a magic spell and soon all the cookie
babies were smiling or crying, waving their
arms or kicking their legs.
"Oh, my," said Wizzo. "Now I've done it! I'll
need twelve dozen baby bottles, twelve dozen
baby beds and I don't know how many diapers!
There's no time to make spells."
So he got out the yellow pages and began
to phone.

Within an hour, the house was filled with babies' bottles, babies' beds, babies' diapers, babies' toys and all the other things babies need... and a new washing machine as well.

Wizzo worked all day and all night looking after those babies. And all the next day and night, and the next.
"Making spells is easy compared to this," he said.

When Ms. Wizzo returned home, Wizzo was
 in the garden hanging out the laundry.
"You didn't meet me," she said.
"Sorry, dear. I was too busy," Wizzo replied.
"And you look worn out. What have you been
doing? And what's all this laundry?"
When Wizzo told her what he had done,
Ms. Wizzo said, "I might have known you'd
get up to something while I was away. Now,
let's see those babies!"

She loved them all.

Wizzo, Ms.Wizzo and Wuff were kept busy all the time for many years until all the babies grew up and left home.

"It's so quiet here," said Wizzo one day.

"Too quiet," his wife agreed.

"It's lonely without them," Wizzo continued.

"Too lonely," his wife replied.

"There's not much to do, now they've gone," said Wizzo.

"Not much at all," sighed his wife.

They looked at each other and smiled.

"Let's make some more cookie babies," suggested Ms. Wizzo.

"Let's make twice as many as before!"

So they set to work, and by the time they had finished, they had made two hundred and eighty-eight cookie babies.

They loved them all!

JAN - - 2008

JUN - - 2011